D0734546

Mystery at Blue Ridge Cemetery

To the generations who grew up with and loved
The Spotlight Club . . . and those of you
who are discovering Jay and Cindy
and Dexter for the first time.

Library of Congress Cataloging-in-Publication Data

Heide, Florence Parry.
Mystery at Blue Ridge Cemetery / by Florence Parry Heide and Roxanne Heide
Pierce ; illustrated by Sophie Escabasse.
pages cm
Summary: "What does the long-deceased Serafina Winslow have to do with the
disappearance of a valuable locket? Leave it to the Spotlight Club to dig up the
answers!"—Provided by publisher.
[1. Mystery and detective stories. 2. Cemeteries—Fiction. 3. Clubs—Fiction.] I. Pierce,
Roxanne Heide. II. Escabasse, Sophie, illustrator. III. Title.
PZ7.H36Myb 2013
[Fic]—dc23
2012032690

10 9 8 7 6 5 4 3 2 1 LB 16 15 14 13 12

Cover and interior illustrations by Sophie Escabasse.

For information about Albert Whitman & Company,
visit our web site at www.albertwhitman.com.

Contents

Mystery at
Blue Ridge Cemetery

FLORENCE PARRY HEIDE AND
ROXANNE HEIDE PIERCE

Albert Whitman & Company
Chicago, Illinois

CHAPTER 1

A Ghost of a Story

A SHARP GUST of wind suddenly rustled the thin paper Cindy Temple had taped to a tombstone in the Blue Ridge Cemetery.

"Hey!" she said, laughing. "Must be a ghost!"

She and her brother, Jay, were with their best friend and next-door neighbor, Dexter Tate. Cindy and Jay were blond and freckled while Dexter was dark-haired and wore glasses. The three had their own club, the Spotlight Club, and called themselves the Spotlighters. They'd solved many mysteries in the past, and it had been months since they'd had a real one. They were itching for something new.

Today they were doing stone rubbings. It was a breezy, warm day at the end of May, a perfect day for their project. They hoped to sell their rubbings for the next day's big neighborhood sale. What they really hoped for was to make money. Not for themselves, but for the local museum, which was in real trouble. They'd already done several a piece and were working on their last ones.

"This is kind of tricky," Dexter said, trying to keep his own paper taped to his chosen tombstone. "But fun." They each had a broad, flat pencil that they carefully ran over the paper. Images appeared, almost ghostly, as they worked.

"Here, listen to this," Jay said. "This is on Jacob Wendover's stone: 'At last' I'm gone. All rejoice. It's true, I've finally lost my voice.'"

"But that's funny," Cindy said. "Who would put something funny on a tombstone?"

"Why not?" asked Dexter. "I think it's a great idea. Why should there be just gloom and doom? I think for my tombstone it should say, 'Here lies Dex, on a whim. There was nothing wrong with him.'"

A Ghost of a Story

Cindy laughed at Dexter's good-naturedness. "You're right, she said. "Funny is good." She looked back down at her stone. "I've got Serafina Winslow," she said. "Died in 1862." She paused. "Wow. She was born in 1842—so she died when she was only twenty."

"Awfully young," Jay mused. "Right in the middle of the Civil War." The Spotlighters continued rubbing busily on their stones.

Blue Ridge Cemetery was like a park, Cindy thought. Massive maple trees spread over the sweeping lawns, where sun-bleached tombstones lay in tidy rows among the slopes of grass. Flowers were placed near many of the grave sites, some real, some artificial. If she squinted her eyes, Cindy thought they all looked real. It was a beautiful place to be. In fact, it was one of Cindy's favorite places. Ever since she could remember, her mom had taken her and Jay here for picnics and long walks. When Cindy was older, she went by herself, bringing a book to read. She'd always felt good about being here. But today, for the first time, she sensed unease. Something about the way the trees seemed to bend together, almost as if sharing a secret.

The Spotlighters were lost in their projects when they heard a sudden sneeze behind them. Cindy jumped, and her flat lead pencil flew from her hand.

"Excuse me," a man said. His voice was low, his words clipped. He leaned on his rake as he looked at the Spotlighters. He was lean and tall with short, stubby reddish hair. "What are you doing here?" he asked. Cindy noticed that his eyes were a piercing blue and held a steady gaze.

The Spotlighters introduced themselves and explained that they were doing stone rubbings and were hoping to sell theirs to earn money for the museum fund-raiser the next day.

The man nodded slowly. "I see," he said. He studied their work for a moment and then glanced up at the Spotlighters. "I'm Chuck, by the way," he said. "I'm the groundskeeper here. I like to make sure everything's on the up and up, so to speak. Wouldn't want any vandalizing here," he added pointedly.

"We'd never vandalize," Jay said, feeling his face begin to warm. Chuck waved his hand in the air, as if to shoo a fly away. "Enough said. I believe you. You

4

look like honest kids." He paused and stared off into the distance. "You can never be too sure."

The Spotlighters glanced at one another. "We just want to help the museum," Dexter said.

Chuck blinked and returned his gaze to the Spotlighters, "I heard about the museum troubles," he said. "It's a shame. We need a museum to preserve all the old, wonderful bits and pieces of history." He paused again, staring off into the distance. "There's so much history right here in this cemetery—it goes on and on." He glanced again at the Spotlighters' rubbings. "I'll bet you could get $15 each for those," he said. "People love history."

There was another pause, and Dexter spoke up. "What's groundskeeping? he asked.

Chuck allowed a small smile to escape his still face. "I keep the grounds around here as neat as I can. You know, raking, sweeping, cutting grass, weeding, shoveling in the winter, generally making this cemetery as beautiful as I can. That sort of thing." A few birds chirped in the distance, and the trees rustled in the soft breeze. "It's important for those who visit the graves of

A Ghost of a Story

their loved ones. And important for those same loved ones to be able to roam as they please in a well-taken care of place." A crooked smile played on Chuck's lips.

The Spotlighters' eyes widened. What was Chuck talking about?

"Ghosts?" the Spotlighters said in unison.

Chuck stared at the Spotlighters. "Of course," he said. "They're all over. And since I have a little cottage on the other side of the place, I can keep a close watch on their comings and goings. I'm their biggest fan. I don't doubt that there is some wandering soul here and there, even as we speak." He paused and studied the Spotlighters. "Interested in ghost stories?" he asked, warming to his audience. Cindy noticed that Chuck seemed to get friendlier the more he talked.

"Tell us," she urged, feeling a little bubble of nervous excitement in the pit of her stomach.

"The old theater in town," Chuck began, leaning on his rake. "There was a very dedicated actor, a lead in a play. He never missed a rehearsal—this was about seventy years ago or so—and everyone figured he'd leave the theater here and head to Hollywood. Well, one late afternoon as he was driving to the theater, he was killed by a train. It's been said that ever since that fateful night, he's been showing up at the theater. They say you can hear him repeat his lines."

The hair on the back of Cindy's neck stood up. "Any other stories?" she asked.

"Sure," Chuck said. "There's always a ghost story. The old girls' boarding school on the south side of town is still haunted by a nun who was struck by lightning during a storm while she was returning with the mail. Some say she can be seen crossing the driveway again and again, trying to get the mail inside."

Cindy had a sudden vision of a nun bending into driving rain, drops cascading down her black habit as the wind whipped leaves all around her. "Well," Cindy said, "Ghost stories are good and spooky. But they're just stories."

Chuck looked at the Spotlighters. "Many a skeptic has changed his mind," he said cryptically, twisting the rake handle in his hand. "I've heard unaccounted-for noises here and there. At night. Someone or something is out there...I feel it."

A Ghost of a Story

Cindy looked around at the lovely grounds. She could imagine that in a place like this at night someone alone could feel a little spooked by noises and things. But no, she decided. The stories were fun, exciting to listen to, but real ghosts? The noises Chuck heard now and then were more than likely nighttime animals hunting for food.

"I've never felt unwelcome here," she offered. "I love it here. In fact, I often bring a book to read, where I sit on that old wrought-iron bench over there. Under the willow tree."

Chuck nodded knowingly. "That bench? Quite a treasured piece of art, very valuable. The man who built it is now a very famous artist who made most of his pieces one hundred-fifty years ago—his name is Will Winslow."

"Hey, we know him," Jay said excitedly. "From school. My teacher said Winslow put Kenoska on the map."

"Maybe Kenoska should really be named Winslow," Dexter suggested.

"Winslow," Cindy mused. "That's the same last name of the stone rubbing I'm doing. Serafina Winslow."

"Her father," Chuck said. "I've done lots of studying of some of the Civil War families here. I almost feel as if I know them. The Winslow family is one of them, particularly Will. There's a mystery surrounding what is supposedly his first artistic piece, a delicate ring with the words *Love Lasts* on it. It's been written about countless times, as old records show. Many mentions of it, but no one has ever seen it." He paused. "Ah, but I get carried away." He took a deep breath and let it out with a whistle. "I should listen more closely to the voices at night, find some things out."

"The ghost syndrome again," laughed Jay.

Chuck looked at him, his head tilted. "You shouldn't be so quick to judge," he said. Then he glanced at his watch. "Gotta run. Much to do." He strode off across the grounds, dragging his rake behind him.

The Spotlighters watched him leave. "Interesting guy," Dexter said. "He sure does believe in ghosts,"

"But he doesn't seem too wacky or anything," Jay said. "Just…different."

"I like him," Cindy said. "At first I didn't think he'd talk to us at all, or if he did, he'd just scold us. But he seemed really interested in the cemetery and all the history in it. I hope we see him again."

"We probably will," Dexter said. "Or you will, anyway, considering how much time you spend here with your books."

"You're right," Cindy said. "I want him to tell me more ghost stories if I see him." She looked around her and retrieved her pencil from the grass.

"We should finish our rubbings and get back home," Cindy suggested. "We've got lots to do for tomorrow's fund-raiser before Uncle Dan takes us out for dinner."

When they got back to the Temples', Uncle Dan greeted them with a big hello. He was tall and handsome with wavy auburn hair and a trim mustache. Mrs. Temple's brother always spent a week with them in the summer around Memorial Day.

"How'd the headstone rubbings go?" he asked. "I've never done one myself."

"Frustrating and fun at the same time," Jay said. "The paper was kind of hard to keep in place, but we got some good images. And we met the groundskeeper, who's really interesting."

"He believes in ghosts," added Dexter.

"And he really knows a lot about the Civil War," Cindy said.

"I'd like to meet the guy," said Uncle Dan. "I'm fascinated with the Civil War. And,"—he winked—"ghosts, too."

"Do I hear talk of ghosts?" asked Mrs. Temple as she came into the kitchen. "You know me. Ghost story fanatic."

"We heard a couple of great ghost stories from the Blue Ridge Cemetery groundskeeper today, Mom," said Cindy. "We'll fill you in at dinner at Rattigan's. In the meantime, Jay and Dex and I want to round up all your boxes and help you finish up before tomorrow's sale."

Mrs. Temple smiled. "I can always count on you three to come to the rescue. I'll show you what needs to be done."

Later that evening, after a delicious dinner at Rattigan's and shared conversations about the day, the Spotlighters sat around the kitchen table with their stone rubbings. They'd decided to roll them up and tie them with ribbons.

"Didn't Chuck say we could make about $15 apiece for these?" asked Jay.

"Yep," Dexter said. "Let's cross our fingers."

Just as the last one was tied, Cindy suddenly gasped. "My watch! It's gone!"

"The one Uncle Dan gave you?" asked Jay.

"I know I had it earlier," Cindy said. "I had it at the cemetery, I'm sure."

"Let's check around," Dexter said, pushing his glasses up on his nose. The Spotlighters did a quick search of the rooms in the house. Then they checked Uncle Dan's car.

"Maybe it fell off at the restaurant," Jay suggested. "Let's call and see if someone found it." He found the phone number and dialed it. After a moment, he shook his head. "Nobody turned it in," he said.

"I'll bet it fell off at the cemetery," Cindy said worriedly. "I've just got to go up there and check. Right now."

"Can't it wait?" asked Jay. "We could see much better in the morning."

"I just can't," Cindy said. "There's too much to do in the morning, and I really want to make sure it's there. If you don't want to go, that's fine. I'll go by myself."

"No way. We're going with you," Jay said. He grabbed a flashlight from the kitchen drawer. "It's getting darker by the minute. And the darker it gets, the more ghosts there are!"

CHAPTER 2
On the Case!

THE AIR WAS much cooler now, and Cindy shivered. Was this such a good idea? Maybe they should have waited for the morning. But Cindy was determined. She wanted to find her watch and that's what she was going to do.

Cindy was glad that the cemetery was just a few short blocks from their house. They were walking since Dexter's headlamp had burned out on his bike. They'd have to get it fixed before baby-sitting the Maxwells the next night.

The sidewalk stretched in front of the Spotlighters like a pale snake as their shoes slapped the pavement. None of them felt like talking. The night, still and dark, hung about them like a cloak, and Cindy was grateful for the company. And the flashlight. It shone on nearby trees, their shadows stretching and twisting like live things.

At last they reached the cemetery and began the walk toward the tombstones. Even with the flashlight, they stumbled over unseen tufts of grass and tree roots bulging up from the ground, grotesque and misshapen. A sudden, quick-moving wind darted through the trees, whistling and dancing, pulling at the Spotlighters' hair. It ceased as quickly as it had started, and it was quiet enough to hear faint rustling noises somewhere in the distance.

"What's that?" Jay asked. "That rustling?"

"Probably rabbits or something," Dexter said. "Whatever night animals look for food."

An owl must have seen or heard the Spotlighters, and it sent out chilling, slow hoots.

"The difference between night and day," Cindy whispered.

Finally they saw the spot where they'd been working on their rubbings. They slowly drew closer, Jay shining the flashlight over the tombstones. Something glinted in the flashlight's gleam. "It must be my watch," Cindy cried hopefully.

Before they could reach it, a hoarse whisper cut through the night, "Is that you, Serafina?

The Spotlighters stopped in their tracks so quickly that they bumped into each other. "Let's get out of here!" Jay gulped.

The Spotlighters were out of breath by the time they reached the sidewalk outside the cemetery.

"What happened? What was that?" Jay asked.

Dexter shook his head as he took off his glasses to clean them on his shirt. "We don't believe in ghosts, right? Why did we run?"

"Well, it was scary," Cindy said. "There we were, in the cemetery at night, that crazy owl hooting and the wind acting odd…it was just scary."

The boys laughed nervously. "Yeah, it was scary, that's all," Jay said. "I mean, there's a voice asking if someone dead is there. 'Is that you, Serafina?'" He shook his head.

"Yeah," Dexter said. There was hesitation in his voice. "Wanna go back?"

Jay and Cindy stared at him.

"Go back?" they said in unison.

"Yeah, you know, go back. Prove that it was nothing. Besides, we didn't get your watch."

"Nope," said Jay.

"I'm good," said Cindy. "It's just…we've just been there, and it's really time to go home. We can go back tomorrow."

"Okay," Dexter said, relief in his voice. "Let's go."

Cindy wrapped her arms around herself. "There's a perfectly good explanation," she declared. The Spotlighters found themselves back home, continuing their conversation.

"Hmm," Dexter said. "Whatever it was, I think we could think more clearly if we ate something."

"And I think we could think more clearly if I had my notebook," Cindy said. "We should write down what we know."

"Is this a mystery?" Jay asked. The Spotlighters looked at each other.

"Well, it sure is mystifying," Cindy said. She got her notebook and sat down at the kitchen table, where the

On the Case!

boys joined her. "What do we know?"

Jay said, "We heard a voice in the cemetery."

"Asking about Serafina," Dexter added.

"Who would be in the cemetery at night?" Cindy wondered.

"Well, we were," Jay said.

"Chuck said he sometimes hears noises there at night," Cindy mused.

"Maybe it was Chuck himself," Dexter offered. "Maybe he thought he was seeing Serafina's ghost."

"Okay," Cindy said. "Let's see what we have."

1. **Voice in cemetery**

2. **Who was in cemetery?**

3. **Jay, Cindy, and Dexter were in cemetery.**

<u>**Query:**</u> **Could it be Chuck?**

<u>**Answer:**</u> **Let's ask him after tomorrow's fund-raiser.**

<u>**Query:**</u> **If not Chuck, then who?**

<u>**Answer:**</u> **We don't know because we don't believe in ghosts.**

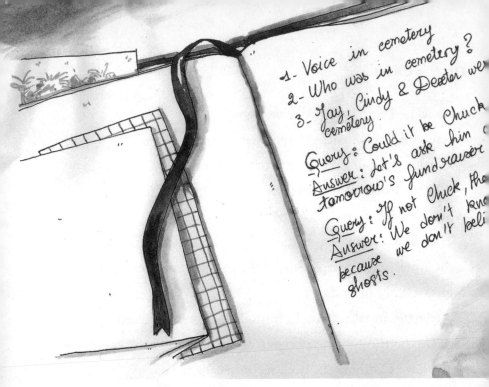

Cindy looked up from her notebook. "Maybe this is the beginning of a mystery."

The next day shone bright and sunny for the museum fund-raiser. The Spotlighters had set up their table with the stone rubbings and other odds and ends. Mrs. Temple and Uncle Dan were busy with a few other card tables on the lawn.

Cindy loved Random Street yard sales, and although this wasn't officially a yard sale in the normal sense, it still brought the neighborhood together. Lots of

20

items were for display on many tables. She saw a few ugly pitchers and smiled when she remembered what Uncle Dan had said, "Remember, beauty is in the eye of the beholder. What's ugly to us may be pretty to someone else. That's what makes the world go round."

Earlier, Uncle Dan had contributed some books to their sale; a few ties; a wallet, used but useful; and a gaudy shirt. "What was I thinking?" he'd asked. "How could I ever have thought such a shirt was handsome?"

Jay, standing next to him at the time, had picked up the shirt, shaken his head, and put the shirt down again. "Well, it does what it was designed to do," he'd said.

That reminded Cindy that Jay had also contributed some personal things to the sale, namely some old comic books as well as an old jacket he'd really liked. "So I've outgrown it," Jay said dejectedly. "It's still the best jacket ever."

"Maybe you could frame it, hang it over the fireplace," Cindy had told him, laughing.

Cindy noted with satisfaction that more and more people were appearing at the fund-raising sale. And not just Random Street neighbors, she thought. That's because everyone wants to help the museum.

"I sure hope we can sell every single stone rubbing," Jay said as he arranged them neatly on a card table.

"Why don't we take turns selling our stuff?" Dexter said. "That way we'll each have a chance to scout around and look at everybody else's things."

"Oh good," said Cindy. "I really want to check some things out. I'll come back in half an hour to take your place."

"I'm going to stay with Dex," Jay said. "I can look around later."

"Okay," Cindy said. She took her wallet out of her shoulder bag and checked to make sure she had the money she had made last week from odd jobs—staying with the Maxwell kids when their parents went to the movies; weeding the Simpsons' garden; picking up Mrs. Anton's prescriptions every week. She had enough money so that she could buy something if it was something she really wanted. She wouldn't buy junk. What Uncle Dan called "jink jank junk."

She'd walked along Random Street many different

times, maybe a million, she thought, but today seemed like a brand new time with neighbors all outside all at the same time. Some she knew, of course, but some were new to her. Good—people she'd never met before, never seen before, could become friends. A stranger is just a friend you've never met before. That's what Uncle Dan always told her. Keep your eyes open. Keep your heart open, he'd said.

Cindy stopped from time to time to look at the various things that people were offering for sale. Some were, as Uncle Dan said, junk. But she did see some pretty and likable things, though she didn't want to buy them.

The main thing about today, she decided, was the feeling of friendliness. She realized that most of the people who lived on Random Street kept to themselves; they didn't walk around greeting each other. Now everyone was smiling, everyone was happy to see one another. This is the way it should always be, she thought. Everyone outside, mingling, liking each other.

At the far end of the street was a house Cindy had

always liked, although she had never seen anyone going in or out, never seen anyone sitting on the porch, even though there were chairs and tables and even a porch swing. It was very, very old, maybe even two hundred years old. And, Cindy noticed, the only house on the street that did not have tables set up to sell things. There were just two garbage cans and a big cardboard box set out for tomorrow's trash pickup.

Cindy looked up at the house again, imagining a third floor attic. Attics can hold many surprising treasures. You never knew what you might find, lost for years and years, hidden away in a box or under something forgotten. Attics were just about Cindy's favorite places. Maybe if she could meet the owner of the house she would be invited to help clean the attic. Then she could see for herself what interesting surprises there were, just waiting to be discovered.

She sighed. Already she was picturing herself up in that attic with mysterious and enchanting secrets. She stood across from the house for a while studying it, wondering what it would be like inside, when the door was flung open and a tall, angular woman stepped out onto the porch. Her hair was black and hung straight, almost touching her shoulders. Black bangs lay across her forehead, straight as a ruler. She wore black jeans and a black T-shirt. A locket hung around her neck. Cindy registered this at the same time she observed the woman's scowling face. Maybe she was mad at something or maybe frowning was her usual expression.

Cindy crossed the street, wondering if she would have the nerve to introduce herself. When she stepped over the curb, she saw that the box set out for trash held old photographs, books, and interesting-looking papers. She approached the woman, readying her face with a smile.

She pointed to the box. "Are you throwing this away?" she asked.

The scowl on the woman's sharp face turned even scowlier. "It's trash, pure and simple," she said. Even her voice was sharp. "Old family garbage. Who needs it? Take it if you want. Take it away."

"Thank you," said Cindy. "I will."

"Well, then, be quick about it," the woman snapped.

"I don't have time to stand around chewing the fat with some nosy kid."

Cindy's face reddened as she bent down to pick up the box. She sure didn't feel like introducing herself to this woman now. Forget the dream of getting a chance to look in her attic. She didn't care if she ever saw her again. It was funny how moods could change so fast—Cindy had just been thinking about the idea that strangers were really just friends you hadn't met yet. This was a woman she could never be friends with!

She hurried down the street with the box, wondering why the woman would be so rude. Whoever she was she certainly had a huge chip on her shoulder.

After Cindy dropped the box off at home, she checked on Jay and Dexter.

"Cindy!" Jay said. "You'll never guess! We sold every last stone rubbing!"

"We made $300!" Dexter crowed.

"Wow," Cindy said, impressed. "We're really going to help the museum!"

"We sure are," agreed Jay. "And now Dex and I can do a tour of the street and see what's out there."

"Sure hope you don't run into a certain nasty lady at the end of the street," Cindy said, shaking her head.

"Ahhh," Jay said. "I think you mean Claudia Somebody. Uncle Dan told us this morning who lives there—and that she always seems to get up on the wrong side of the bed. He knew her growing up in this neighborhood. They're the same age."

"That's Uncle Dan for you," Cindy smiled. "He always puts things in perspective." She pictured that Claudia lady as a little girl, mean even then. How sad that she was still the neighborhood grouch at thirty-five.

CHAPTER 3
A Family Feud

THE SPOTLIGHTERS SPLIT up, each checking different tables along the street. Cindy was drawn across the street to a long buffet table filled with vases and picture frames. She shifted her shoulder bag to her other shoulder and picked up a beautiful picture frame. She turned it over. Did she really need it? She'd think about it. As she set it back down, she heard a sharp voice complaining. "Are you serious? You want to charge me twenty-five cents for this inferior bag? It's worn!"

Cindy didn't have to look twice to know that it was Claudia speaking. But she did look. And something caught her eye. The locket around Claudia's neck was the most interesting locket Cindy had ever seen. It was gold, shaped like a heart, and in beautifully engraved letters were the words Love is the Key. It was almost as if the words were lit from within. Love is the Key, Cindy thought. How romantic. For some reason it seemed strangely familiar. She thought that such a lovely thing was contrary to Claudia's unpleasant personality.

Cindy heard a gasp of surprise—or was it fear?—and saw Claudia's expression turn to anger. As Cindy watched, Claudia reached around her neck and removed the locket. In a single movement, Claudia dropped the necklace into a slender-necked vase on the table and quickly turned away.

What was that about? Cindy wondered. Why did Claudia hide the locket? Because surely, that's what she had done. Deliberately. Who was she hiding it from? It was a mystery, and Cindy was going to find out what was going on. Crowds of people were mingling around the tables, and she jostled around to get a better look at Claudia.

A slender, blond woman approached Claudia, her face bewildered. She looked in shock, Cindy thought.

A Family Feud

"Claudia!" the woman exclaimed. "The locket! You were just wearing the locket that you said has been missing for years! Where is it?"

"What locket?" Claudia asked innocently. "I don't know what you're talking about. I don't have any locket."

Cindy stared. She was lying. What was going on?

"You just had it hanging around your neck!" the blond woman said.

"Carmen," interjected Claudia. "You're seeing things. You always were the sister who made things up, causing a stir. It's clear to me that you're just having one of your episodes."

The blond woman—Carmen—shook her head in disbelief and frustration. Cindy felt a sudden pang of sympathy for her, again determined to find out what this whole thing was about. At least she'd figured out that the two women were sisters.

Claudia was edgy, Cindy could tell. Just as she wondered whether or not she should speak up about where the locket really was, she and Claudia turned at the same time to look at the vase where Claudia had dropped the locket. It was gone.

Claudia's eyes darted to Cindy's, black with rage.

"Stop, thief!" she shouted at Cindy, pointing her thin finger at Cindy's face.

Cindy blinked. Did Claudia think she'd taken the locket? Or the vase?

Claudia reached over to Cindy, clutching at Cindy's shoulder bag. "Empty it!" she hissed. By now the people who had been browsing nearby stopped to observe what was going on.

Her face burning, Cindy turned her bag upside down and dumped it out. Claudia rummaged through the contents. "I'm not finished with you," she muttered angrily.

Carmen hurriedly came between her sister and Cindy. "I apologize for my sister's behavior," she said, obviously distraught. "This is just terrible." She turned to Claudia. "Please apologize to this girl."

"I'll do no such thing," Claudia sneered. She turned to Cindy. "You'll be sorry," she said as she spun away and hurried down the street.

Carmen helped Cindy return her things to her bag. "I am so sorry," she said. "Claudia has always had a temper.

A Family Feud

I haven't seen her in a long time, and I came to town to try to make amends, try to smooth our relationship out." She shook her head. "But I see that she's not ready."

The people who'd watched the incident moved on to other tables. Cindy was torn between telling Carmen about the locket in the vase and wanting to tell Jay and Dexter first. Carmen seemed like a good person, and Cindy wanted to help her. She decided she needed to talk to the boys first.

"By the way," Carmen said with a small smile, "I'm Carmen Wells." She held out her hand to Cindy.

"I'm Cindy Temple," Cindy said as she shook Carmen's hand. "I live across the street, over there." She nodded at her house.

Just then Dexter and Jay showed up. "What was the commotion all about?" Jay asked. "Dex and I heard shouting."

"My sister was rude to Cindy," Carmen said after she introduced herself. "Claudia was out of line, and I apologize for her."

Cindy shook her head. "It's okay," she said. "Let's just forget about it." But she knew she would not forget and very much wanted to talk to the boys about the locket.

"Hope to see you again," Carmen said with a smile. And then a dark cloud passed over her face. Cindy knew she was thinking of the locket.

Carmen shook herself. "Well, time to get going." She nodded at the Spotlighters and turned to walk down Random Street.

CHAPTER 4
The Missing Locket

CINDY COULD HARDLY speak fast enough. "We've got a real mystery," she said with both excitement and anger. "Claudia was wearing a locket, and when Carmen saw it, Claudia took it off and dropped it into a vase, and—"

"Whoa, slow down," Jay said. "What are you talking about?"

"Okay," Cindy said, forcing herself to slow down.

"I saw Claudia—you know, the mean lady—and she was wearing a locket, really pretty and unusual. And then she suddenly took it off and dropped it into a brass vase on a table."

"Why'd she do that?" asked Dexter.

"Because she saw Carmen coming," Cindy said. "And she didn't want her to know she had the locket."

"So she hid it," Jay concluded.

"Exactly," Cindy said. "And then...then she accused me of stealing it and made me empty my bag on the table."

"Wait a minute," Dexter said with a frown. "Didn't you just say the locket was in the vase?"

Cindy nodded. "It was. But somebody must have bought it a minute before. It was there, and then it wasn't."

"So, let me get this straight," Dexter continued. "Claudia was wearing this locket. She sees Carmen, panics, takes it off, and hides it from her sister. The vase with the locket suddenly vanishes, and Claudia thinks you had something to do with it."

"Yes," Cindy said. "It was really humiliating."

"I think we should spread out and look for anyone carrying a vase," suggested Jay. "Whoever bought it could still be here, looking for other things to buy."

"I agree," Dexter said. "Let's go, Jay." The boys took

off, and Cindy stood for a moment, looking at the remaining vases on the table. Who could have bought it? If only she'd seen something.

Just on the off-chance that she'd made a mistake about which vase the locket was in, Cindy pretended she was interested in buying one. She lifted them up, one by one, and turned them upside down. Nothing. Maybe the boys would find the person who bought the vase.

Cindy thought about Claudia. The woman was mean and spiteful, but was there more to her than that? What was the real motive behind hiding the locket? She remembered how Claudia acted when Cindy took the box from the curb. And that reminded her of the box itself and what its contents held.

Suddenly Cindy wanted to see just what was in that box. She hurried home, greeted her mom and Uncle Dan, and got the box. She settled herself on the living room couch, the contents of the box dumped out around her. A musty smell rose up, and to Cindy it was not an unpleasant odor. It reminded her of attics. She wondered if this box had been in that attic she'd dreamed of visiting earlier—before Carmen appeared and acted so mean. This was the kind of thing Cindy loved to look at. There were old photographs and newspaper clippings, a few books. She picked one up at random and noted that the pages were yellowed and brittle. She felt right at home with these old relics and wondered about the people who had read them.

Cindy sifted through the papers and saw another book with a broken clasp. She opened it and saw that it wasn't a book after all but some kind of journal. Sketches of all kinds filled half the pages, and the handwriting looked old-fashioned, the letters sleek and uniformly styled. Cindy read a passage: "Papa says that if I do all my lessons for the week I shall be able to attend the Southport League Ball. I will surely finish my lessons, for I should not want to miss the ball for anything. I have a new petticoat to wear under my green dress, and although my good shoes are old, I can shine them up with paste. And oh, I do believe Charles Headly will attend!"

Cindy felt oddly connected to this voice from the past and was eager to read more. The outside world—

The Missing Locket

and the memory of Claudia's confrontation—faded into the background.

Who was this person? Cindy wondered. She leafed to the front of the journal to look for a name.

In a bold scrawl was the name Serafina Winslow.

Cindy stared, then blinked. There was no mistaking the name. The very name on the tombstone that she had used for her last rubbing! She felt a cold chill pass through her as she remembered the hoarse voice calling, "Is that you, Serafina?"

She wondered at the coincidence. Eager to read more, Cindy turned to a passage farther in the journal. "I am to prepare a meal for eight tomorrow, and I am unhinged. Papa says to pay attention to Mama's old recipes. But she could cook! I shall make a mess of everything, I am sure of it."

A page later, Cindy read, "I did what Mama's recipes said to do, but I burnt the potatoes and undercooked the lamb. Papa said everything was delicious, and he rewarded me with a new bracelet he made. Everything he makes is beautiful. I shall always think of burnt potatoes when I wear it."

As Cindy flipped through more pages, she saw sketches of flowers, chipmunks, trees…and to Cindy's astonishment, a drawing of the very locket she had seen Claudia hide in the brass vase this morning. There were the words, *Love is the Key*, inscribed on the locket. It was drawn so well that it looked real.

Beneath the drawing Serafina had written, "The most beautiful locket in the world! Papa gave it to me today for my sixteenth birthday. When opened, it holds a picture of Papa. He is so handsome! I shall treasure it

The Missing Locket

forever. It holds a wonderful secret, he says, which will be revealed to me later. He loves to speak of secrets. He told me of another secret, one he's held in his heart since he was hardly older than myself. About something dear to his heart that he created. In a circle, he said, and all about love. Whatever can he mean by that?"

While Cindy continued to read the journal, Jay and Dexter searched the Random Street neighborhood for anyone who might be carrying a vase.

Suddenly Jay grabbed Dexter's arms. "Look," he said. "That man."

Dexter pushed his glasses down on his nose. "What man? And what about him? Where?"

Jay pointed. "The man in the blue jacket. Right over there. He's carrying a vase. That's got to be the one with the locket in it."

"And maybe he doesn't even know there's a locket in it," Dexter suggested.

"He'll soon find out. Or should we tell him? Or is it even our business?" worried Jay. "Why did Claudia want to hide the locket from Carmen, anyway? And does she know that man has the vase?"

"But she was so sure that Cindy had it, remember?" Dexter reasoned.

"Well, whatever and whoever and however and whichever, we have to find out more. Let's follow him."

"Exactly," Dexter said. "Hey, look! He's going into Florence's Flower Shop. Let's wait outside and see what happens."

"We can look in the window and pretend we're just admiring the flowers," suggested Jay. "We don't want him to suspect that we're following him."

In a few minutes the man stepped out of the flower shop holding the vase, which was now filled with flowers.

"And he still doesn't know there's a locket in there?" asked Jay.

"Or does he? Maybe he's known all along," Dexter wondered. "Let's see where he's going with that vase."

They stayed well behind him and kept him in sight.

"He's heading to Blue Ridge Cemetery," Jay said.

"He's going to put those flowers at a grave," Dexter decided. "In memory of someone who's buried there."

Jay nodded thoughtfully. "Or maybe not. Maybe he's planning to leave the vase for someone to pick up later."

"Wish Cindy was with us," sighed Jay.

"You can say that again," Dexter said.

"Wish Cindy was with us" Jay laughed. "And it's true: three detectives are better than two."

"The man is looking at tombstones," Dexter whispered. "Let's watch to see which one he leaves his flowers next to."

The two detectives watched as the man walked around the cemetery.

"He doesn't know we're watching him," Jay said softly.

"That's because we know how to see without being seen," Dexter told him. "One of the tricks of the Spotlight Club."

Suddenly the man stopped and looked behind him.

"Pretend we're looking at a tombstone," whispered Jay.

The two boys leaned over to look at a tombstone and pretended to examine it. "John P. Whitehouse,"

43

Dexter said aloud. "That's the one." He cleared his throat. "Yessir, that's the one."

"It's okay," Jay whispered. "You can stop sounding important. The guy's walking on."

The boys kept pretending to look at various stones.

Dexter looked up and grabbed Jay's arm. "He's coming our way," he said hoarsely.

Sure enough, the man approached them, carrying the vase with flowers. "Excuse me," he said as he drew closer. "I wonder if you could help me. I'm looking for a grave, the grave of Mary Jane Daley. I want to leave these flowers, but I can't find her tombstone. I believe it to be next to three or four graves of the Longhorn family."

Dexter swallowed. He felt foolish for suspecting the man of doing anything questionable. "I don't know where those graves are, but I'll help," he said.

"You bet," added Jay. "If it's here, we'll find it."

And indeed, in a few minutes the boys had located the grave of Mary Jane Daley. The man thanked them, and they watched as he placed the vase with the flowers next to the headstone. When he left, he nodded at the boys.

Once he was out of sight, Dexter said, "Okay, let's check the vase."

Jay picked it up, lifted the flowers out, and felt down to the bottom. He shook his head. "Nothing," he said and replaced the flowers. "No locket, no anything." He paused. "Wait a minute," he said slowly. "So the locket isn't in this vase when we thought it might be. That's not the end of the story. *Or* the mystery. The locket is somewhere, just not here."

"We'll just have to keep our eyes open," Dexter said.

"Let's find Cindy," Jay said.

"Right," Dexter agreed. "Let's tell her every single thing we know about what we've seen."

And the boys started home to find Cindy.

CHAPTER 5
Serafina's Journal

CINDY WAS STILL riveted by her discovery of Serafina's journal and in particular the sketch of the locket drawn here that Claudia was so desperate to hide from Carmen…what was the connection? And where were Jay and Dexter when she needed them? She needed to talk to them about her discoveries. She put the journal and books and papers back in the box and went to look for the boys.

Just as Cindy reached the front door, the boys burst in.

"There you are!" Jay said excitedly.

"And there you are!" said Cindy. "I need to tell you what I've found."

"And we need to tell you what we did," Dexter added.

"We followed a man to the cemetery," Jay went on. "He had a vase. We were sure it was the one with the locket in it."

"But the locket wasn't there," Dexter said.

"It was a mistake," Jay finished.

"So it all turned out to be a red herring," Cindy concluded.

"Yep," said Jay. "A false clue, a false lead, we just made a mistake, thinking the man had the locket."

"Red herring," mused Dexter. "Where did that expression come from, anyway? I know what it means but that's all I know. I know it means following a false clue."

"I remember reading something about it somewhere," Cindy said. "In England, people would train their hunting dogs by dragging a red herring—a fish—over the fields to distract the dogs so they would learn to follow the fox scent. So I guess it's really a distraction, something that just throws you off the track."

"Heh," Dexter said. "Off the right track is right, that's for sure."

"But you didn't know that," Cindy said. "You pursued that man, thinking he was the real thing." She shook her head. "Every part to a mystery counts, false leads or not. They keep us on our toes."

Jay and Dexter nodded. "That makes me feel better," Jay said.

"Me too," Dexter added.

"Hey!" Cindy said. "My turn! I found Serafina Winslow's journal, and in it is a drawing of the very same locket Claudia was wearing and then hid in the vase."

Dexter and Jay stared at Cindy. "The same locket?" Jay asked.

"The very same," Cindy said excitedly.

"This is really getting interesting," Dexter said. "I wonder what—"

Just then the doorbell rang. Cindy opened the door, and there stood Carmen, Cindy's notebook in her hand.

"Hi, Cindy," she said warmly as she handed the notebook to her. "This must have fallen off the table this morning after…after Claudia made you empty your bag. I knew where you lived, and I wanted to get it back to you."

"Thank you so much," Cindy said gratefully. Then she quickly glanced at the boys and returned her gaze

to Carmen. "We have something to tell you," she said urgently. "Please come in."

Carmen looked bewildered but followed the Spotlighters into the living room where they all sat down.

"I saw the locket that you and Claudia were arguing about," Cindy began.

"You did?" Carmen asked, startled. "Where did you see it?"

"Around her neck," Cindy said. "And then when she saw you coming, she took it off and dropped it into a nearby vase on one of those tables."

"And bang, somebody must have bought the vase before anybody noticed," Dexter said.

"That's when Claudia made me empty my bag," Cindy offered.

"And then Dex and I saw some guy with a vase and decided to keep an eye on him. In case," Jay said.

"And we followed him, waited, watched...but no locket after all," Dexter added.

Carmen looked from one Spotlighter to the other, speechless, her eyes wide.

"There's more," Cindy said excitedly. "I picked up a box of things from Claudia's curb," she went on. "She wasn't selling anything, but she had put things out for trash pick up. She said I could take the box. And when I got a chance to look in it, there was a journal of Serafina Winslow's, with a drawing of that very same locket."

Carmen gasped.

The Spotlighters looked at each other and then back at Carmen.

"So much information!" she exclaimed. "I can hardly absorb it all. You said you found Serafina's journal?" she asked Cindy.

Cindy nodded.

"That's family property!" Carmen cried.

"Family property?" Cindy echoed.

Carmen nodded, her hands twisting in her lap. "Serafina Winslow is our ancestor."

It was Cindy's turn to gasp. "You're related to Serafina?" she asked, shocked by the coincidence of her picking that particular tombstone for rubbing.

"Yes," Carmen said. "It's been a long-time hope that Claudia would honor our family name—after all, Will Winslow is a national treasure. But for some reason, she has turned her back on me over the years." She paused. "And that locket that she told me had gone missing years ago...she had it all this time." Her face clouded over. "And now to see it and then have it missing again . . ."

"We're going to help you," Cindy interrupted firmly.

"We're detectives," Jay said. "We've solved lots of mysteries. Spotlight Club at your service."

"You can count on us to do everything we can to find out where the locket is and return it to you," Dexter said.

Carmen looked at the Spotlighters. "I believe you," she said gratefully. "I can't think how you could ever find it, but I—I thank you." She blinked her eyes and smiled at each of the Spotlighters. She glanced at her watch. "I've got an appointment...but here"— she reached into her purse and pulled out a small card—"In case you need to reach me," she said. "And thank you again, all of you," she said as she stood up.

The Spotlighters showed her out and told her not to worry. She lifted a hand in good-bye and left.

"We definitely have a mystery," Dexter said.

"Thank heavens for my notebook," Cindy said. "Let's write down what we know." She glanced at the boys. "Mystery of the Missing Locket?"

The boys nodded.

"Okay," Cindy said. She readied herself with her notebook and a pencil.

Query: Why did Claudia hide the locket from Carmen?

Answer: Because she wanted it.

Query: Who took the vase with the locket in it?

Answer: We don't know.

"Pretty much a dead end," Jay said. "What else have we got?"

"Well," Cindy said. "We have a name, Serafina Winslow...and we also have her journal."

"And who was she?" Dexter asked.

"What we know is that she was the daughter of the famous artisan, Will Winslow," Cindy said, writing notes. "She had a locket—the missing one—with the words *Love is the Key* made by her father for her sixteenth birthday." She tapped her pencil on her notebook. "He has lots of art pieces all over Kenoska, worth tons of money."

"Maybe Claudia wanted the locket because it's so valuable," Jay suggested.

"Maybe," considered Jay. "But then why would she be wearing it instead of trying to sell it?"

"Maybe she's sentimental," suggested Cindy. Then she started to laugh and had a coughing fit. "Just kidding," she finally managed.

Jay laughed with Cindy and then said, "We need to concentrate on where the locket could possibly be. We never found anybody with a vase, so somebody is out there with it. And the locket."

"Needle in a haystack," Dexter sighed. "I say we eat something and stand back from this a little. Maybe we should bike up to the cemetery to look for Cindy's watch."

"You're right, Dex," Cindy said. "We need a change of scene."

CHAPTER 6
Ghosts Are Everywhere

IN MOMENTS, THE Spotlighters had grabbed some snacks and biked to the cemetery. Cindy couldn't help thinking about the night before and the eerie voice that had seemed to come out of nowhere. The boys seemed to share her thoughts. "Wow, what a difference between night and day," Jay said.

"That's exactly what I said last night," Cindy said. "It really is amazing how different it can be!"

They once again headed to the area where they'd been before to do their stone rubbings.

After searching around in the grass and looking everywhere, Cindy said dejectedly, "It's not here after all. I can't imagine where I lost it."

In spite of their coming up with nothing, Jay and Dexter continued looking, spreading out farther from the tombstones. They were about to give up when they heard a familiar voice behind them.

"Back again, I see," said Chuck. "Going to do more stone rubbings?"

"Not today," Cindy said, "We're actually here to look for my watch. I thought it must have fallen off here."

"Well," said Chuck in his clipped voice. "I did find a watch here when I was doing my routine checking of the grounds. Perhaps it's yours."

"You have it?" Cindy asked excitedly.

"Well, if it's silver with turquoise hands, yes," Chuck said. Cindy's face lit up when he took it out of his pocket and showed it to her. "That's it!" she exclaimed. "I won't wear it again until I've got the clasp fixed," she vowed.

"By the way," Jay said, "we came back here last night to look for the watch, and we distinctly heard someone whisper, 'Is that you, Serafina?' and we wondered who could possibly have said that."

"We didn't stick around to see who it was," Dexter added.

Ghosts Are Everywhere

"Right," Cindy said. "We left in a hurry." She remembered hearing that ghostly voice and the shivers that ran down her spine. But mostly she remembered how eerie the night seemed with the wind and the owl. It had been a strange night.

"There's got to be some explanation," Jay said.

Chuck studied the Spotlighters, his eyes as blue and steady as ever. "There is an explanation," he said. "I was here. I thought I heard Serafina wandering around, and I just thought I'd ask."

"You really do believe in ghosts?" Cindy breathed.

Chuck was silent for a moment. "I was sure I made that clear before," he said, looking at Cindy. "Yes, I believe in ghosts."

Cindy shook her head. "I'm still surprised," she said. "It seems like something right out of a book."

"Don't be so surprised," Chuck said levelly. "There are lots of folks like me."

Cindy couldn't wait to tell Uncle Dan. She could hear him now. "To each his own" or "Different strokes for different folks."

A sudden change seemed to come over Chuck.

It was as though he wanted to reach out to the Spotlighters, to shake off his distance, as though he wanted to share. "There's something I wanted to show you kids the other day, but I ran out of time," he said, "That bench that Cindy likes to read on," he went on. "Bet you never found Will Winslow's initials, did you?"

Cindy shook her head. "I never thought to look," she admitted. "I'd love to now."

In a minute, Chuck and the Spotlighters were at the bench. A huge willow tree stood over it, shading it from the bright sun. The bench was beautifully designed, with leaves twining around and around each other.

Chuck encouraged the Spotlighters to explore the bench. Cindy remembered dozens of times sitting here, letting her hand drift over the sides of the bench as she read. Now, as she studied more closely, she noted a detail she'd missed all the times before. Two hearts, looking like leaves, seemed intertwined. How romantic, she thought.

"Here!" Jay suddenly called. "Over here!" He

pointed to an area on the back of the bench. There were two spidery *W*s next to each other, almost interlocked.

"There you go!" Chuck said encouragingly. "They're on every single piece that he did," he said. "His work is all over the country, but nowhere as much as it is in Kenoska." He nodded to a sleek hitching post just yards away from the bench. "There's another example."

The Spotlighters looked at the hitching post, its head the shape of a horse's head, gleaming and black. A ring was attached to its nose. Cindy remembered seeing a dozen of these hitching posts throughout the cemetery in the past, and again she admired the sleekness and realistic look of the horses' heads.

"Back in those old days," Chuck said, "folks'd ride their horses to this cemetery and hitch right up. Or they'd bring their carriages." He paused. "It must have been beautiful."

Cindy could picture it…the girls and ladies with their heavy skirts and parasols, the men and boys in their stiff, high-collared shirts visiting the tombstones

of families. She loved to think that people long ago had sat on her favorite bench. Maybe kids her own age? Who were they? Did they have thoughts like hers? She felt connected. It made her want to return to Serafina's journal.

"Well, it's time for me to get back to work." Chuck said matter-of-factly.

"We should head back too," Jay said. "I've got a paper route."

"I'll help," said Dexter.

"Thanks for my watch," Cindy said.

Chuck nodded.

"I'm glad you told us it was you calling to Serafina," Dexter said. "We like to figure things out. We're detectives, you know."

"Oh?" asked Chuck, seeming interested. "I'll keep that in mind." He nodded again and headed off across the lawns.

CHAPTER 7

The New Rule

WHEN THE BOYS went off to deliver newspapers, Cindy got Serafina's journal out of the box and settled herself on the living room couch. She leafed through a few pages and was astonished to see a drawing of the cemetery bench. First the locket, now the bench. What an amazing coincidence. Wasn't it?

Or was it? Cindy thought for a minute. Serafina's father was Will Winslow, the man who had created these things...why wouldn't Serafina draw them? She would, Cindy thought, especially since drawing had seemed to come so easily to her. So, there was no mystery there, just a welcome surprise.

There were several different sketches of the bench, some close-ups, some of the whole bench from different angles. There were the intertwining leaves, the intricate details of the vines. Cindy read, "Here's the bench—how I love the bench!—Papa told me that it is a very special piece, even more special than just for sitting on. He loves to pose riddles." There was a long line with an arrow at the end, which pointed to a drawing of the two intertwined hearts Cindy had seen on the bench earlier.

"These hearts are special, Papa says," Cindy read. "Perhaps they stand for Papa and me. He loves hearts—look at the heart locket he made me. He made something else, he told me. Long, long ago, but I have never seen it. He told me that he had a feeling about the future, that no one knows for sure who or what will be the answer, but that someone or something will. What a dear heart. And that reminds me again of this locket." That made Cindy want to revisit the drawing of the locket. She turned a few pages, and as she did, she noticed a drawing she hadn't seen before. It was of the locket seen sideways, thin and sleek. Cindy wondered why Serafina had chosen such a view.

"Papa has told me part of the secret to my locket," Cindy read. "'Think, my Sera, of what is written on this locket. *Love is the Key.* What is a key's purpose?' I am thinking and thinking of what he could mean. I will think some more."

Cindy frowned. There was something in that passage that tugged at her, but she couldn't think what. She turned the page. "When I figure out the secret, Papa says that things will have come full circle. I do not know what that means."

Full circle. An answer to things, Cindy thought. The answer to a riddle, for instance. Something coming back to the beginning. Serafina said her father loved riddles. Perhaps the bench was part of a riddle.

Cindy closed the journal and leaned back against the sofa. She needed to think for a moment. She felt disconnected from the present and closed her eyes, imagining the sights and sounds of the long-ago days of Serafina Winslow.

When Jay and Dexter came bounding into the house an hour later, Cindy realized she'd fallen asleep. She rubbed her eyes and blinked a few times. She'd dreamed of riding in a carriage and wearing layers and layers of clothing. She glanced down at her shorts and shirt and laughed.

"What's so funny?" Jay asked when he came into the living room, Dexter close on his heels.

"Oh, a funny dream I had," Cindy said. "I was reading Serafina's journal…" she trailed off. "But hey, seriously, there was something she wrote down that got me thinking. Her father asked her what the purpose of a key is—like the locket with *Love is the Key* on it. I was just wondering what that means."

"Maybe it means that love is the key that unlocks the love in someone's heart," Jay said.

"That's pretty romantic," Dexter said.

"Well, I'm a pretty romantic guy," Jay said. "Underneath my tough exterior."

Dexter and Cindy rolled their eyes.

"This locket," Cindy said. "There's something more to it than we're seeing."

"Or not seeing," Jay said. "Where is it, anyway? Somebody's got it."

"Why don't we go up and down the street asking

people if they bought a vase at the yard sale?" Dexter suggested.

Cindy stared at Dexter. "That's so simple it might just work," she said. "Can't believe we didn't think of it."

"Let's split up and get going," Jay said excitedly. "This could be it."

"People are so friendly around here," Cindy said. Except, she thought, people like Claudia. Thinking of her made her shudder. And think of why she wanted the locket so badly she had to hide it. "Yeah, it can't hurt," Dexter said. "And we did promise Carmen that we'd do everything we could to help find it."

Within moments, the Spotlighters had assigned themselves different houses, and off they went on foot. They agreed to meet back at the Temples' in an hour.

They started out with great hopes, but by the time their hour was up, none of them had come closer to finding the vase than they had before. Dejectedly, they met back in the kitchen at the Temples'.

"Well, that was a bust," Dexter said.

"Another dead end," Jay sighed.

"It's out there somewhere," Cindy said. "And we're

going to find it." She paused. "And it's not just finding the locket itself...there's more to it than that. I feel it in my bones."

"There's always more to things than you first think," Jay mused. "I think we've found that out with every mystery we've ever solved."

"Good point," Dexter said. "Maybe it's time for a new rule. Something like, Keep Looking—There's More Than Meets the Eye."

Cindy laughed. "It's not like our other rules, but I like it," she said. "Not like Hooley's Rule or the Beaker Trick."

"Or the Usher Rule," Jay added. "I always liked that one. Just because you like somebody doesn't mean you can't suspect him."

"My favorite is Hooley's Rule," Dexter said. "Just because you have a million dollars hidden in your basement doesn't mean for certain that you're the one who stole it."

"I like them all," Cindy said. "Including our new one, the Keep Looking Rule," she added. "I have time to write that one down in my notebook before we leave to baby-sit for Randy and Amy Maxwell."

"And time for a quick snack," Dexter added, helping himself to an apple in a bowl on the kitchen counter.

"I love having a new rule," Cindy said. "How does this sound? 'Keep Looking—There's More Than Meets the Eye.' When you think you've figured everything out, think again."

"It's good," Jay said. "I'll bet we'll be using it in this new mystery."

Cindy nodded thoughtfully. "And I'll bet you're right," she said.

It was about an hour from dusk when the Spotlighters left on their bikes for the Maxwells'. Cindy was glad that Dexter had gotten his headlamp fixed earlier. Although it wasn't dark now, it would be when they were finished with their baby-sitting job.

They loved Amy and Randy and always had a good time with them. Mrs. Maxwell was spending the night at her sister's house, and Mr. Maxwell had a meeting to attend for an hour. It would be an easy job for just an hour. Then why did Cindy feel so anxious?

She kept looking behind her and off to the side.

The New Rule

"Everything okay?" Jay asked.

"Actually, I feel exposed," Cindy said.

"What do you mean?" asked Dexter. "Exposed to what?"

"I can't put my finger on it," Cindy said. "It's like someone's there but not. I think I see someone behind a tree or bush and when I look again, I don't see anyone."

Jay and Dexter looked around them. "I don't see anyone," Jay offered.

"Me neither," said Dexter.

"That doesn't mean someone isn't there," said Cindy.

"Like who?" asked Jay.

"Like Claudia," Cindy said. "She did say she wasn't through with me."

"Let's just get to the Maxwells' and worry about Claudia later," Dexter said.

When Cindy and Jay and Dexter reached the house, Randy and Amy were standing on the porch waving at them.

"Can you stay for eleventeen days?" asked Amy, jumping up and down.

"Well, we can stay for a while," laughed Cindy, lifting Amy up. "Where's your dad?"

"He's inside getting ready for a meeting," Randy offered importantly. "He has to bring a briefcase and everything."

"Hmm," mused Dexter. "Sounds pretty important."

Randy nodded seriously. "It's about ducks."

"Ducks?" Cindy asked.

"Yep," answered Randy. "Daddy has to get them all in a row. Sometimes they don't like to line up."

"Ducks quack," Amy added as she pulled on Cindy's arm, trying to drag her inside.

"Okay, okay, I'm coming," Cindy laughed. Just as the kids and the Spotlighters walked in the door, Mr. Maxwell appeared.

"Good to see you," he greeted Jay, Cindy, and Dexter. "Randy and Amy have been bouncy all evening waiting for you." He glanced at his watch. "Gotta run. I'll be home no later than an hour. Thanks again. By the way, could you keep the kids in tonight? I think Amy's coming down with something, and I'd rather she be tucked in."

The New Rule

"Of course," Cindy said, ruffling Amy's hair.

"I'm not coming down, Dad," Amy said. "I'm coming *up!*" And she jumped up to prove it.

The Spotlighters laughed, and Mr. Maxwell patted Amy on the head. "Okay, angel."

"Good luck with your ducks, Dad," Randy said.

"Thanks, son," Mr. Maxwell said with a smile.

After he'd left, the children started talking at once about what game they wanted to play.

"Flowers in the pot!" screeched Amy.

"Marching!" insisted Randy.

"Flowers in the pot!"

"Marching!"

"Whoa!" laughed Jay. "Maybe we can do both marching and flowers in the pot, what do you say?"

"'Kay, if we can do flowers in the pot first," Amy said.

"Fine," said Cindy. "But you'll have to tell us how to play it. Marching I understand—and we'll do that too, Randy, I promise. But explain the flower game, Amy."

"First, you take the pot Mommy buyed and you find some flowers to put in it. Then you take it to the subutary." Amy radiated good cheer.

The Spotlighters stared blankly at Amy.

"Subutary," mused Dexter, scratching his head. "That's a new one."

"She means cemetery," Randy explained. "She's not real good at long words yet 'cuz she's only two."

"Cemetery. . ." Cindy said. "What about the cemetery?"

"Flowers in the pot!" screeched Amy again.

"Mom got a vase at the yard sale the other day," Randy explained. "She put some flowers in it, and she took us up to the cemetery where she put it at a grave." Randy was clearly finished. He wanted to move on to marching.

Cindy, Jay, and Dexter gaped at Randy.

"Your mom bought a vase at the yard sale?" Cindy asked, feeling her heart pound faster. "And took it to the cemetery?" She exchanged quick glances with Jay and Dexter. They were as excited as she was.

"Yep," Randy answered. "Can we play now?"

"In just a minute," Cindy said hurriedly. "What did the vase look like?"

Randy frowned. "A vase," he said.

The New Rule

Amy piped up, antsy. "Horsey! The horsey can play too."

"Hold on, Amy," Randy said. "I'm telling stuff." He looked back at Cindy. "It was shiny. It had a big bottom and a skinny neck."

Cindy recalled the vase. Yes, it was as Randy described it. She could hardly contain herself. Mrs. Maxwell must have been the one who purchased the vase in that split second. She looked at the boys. They were thinking the same thing.

"And the horsey wanted the flowers," Amy said. "For a snack. But I said no."

The Spotlighters turned to Randy for an explanation.

"Mom took the vase with the flowers in it and set it on a grave near one of those whatchamacallits— you know, those things where you tie up your horse in cowboy movies? There's a bunch of them in the cemetery."

Of course. Those magnificent hitching posts made by Will Winslow—they were just admiring them earlier today!

Jay, Cindy, and Dexter stared at each other. This had to be it. The vase with the locket in it was sitting at a grave, next to a hitching post, in the cemetery that very moment!

Suddenly there was a thump from outside.

"What was that?" Randy asked.

"Nothing, I'm sure," Jay said quickly. But he looked at Cindy and Dexter. Was Cindy right that someone—Claudia—was following them? Was Claudia out there now, listening in on their conversation? After all, the windows were all open, letting the fresh May air into the house. Had she heard about the vase with the locket in it being in the cemetery?

"Time to march!" said Randy. "Amy's turn is up!"

"Okay, we'll march," Cindy said, suggesting with a movement of her head that Jay go check outside. He nodded, and she and Dexter started marching in place. Amy squealed with delight as Randy importantly swung his elbows high while he marched in place too.

Jay slid quietly out the back door while Cindy and Dexter occupied the children. He tiptoed down the three back steps to the yard, being careful not to make

74

The New Rule

a sound. He was certain that the thump had come from the front of the house—and that's where the living room was, where they'd had the conversation about the vase in the cemetery. Had Claudia been listening in? Jay made his way around to the front of the house where the porch was, his back as close to the house as he could manage. Stealthily, slowly, he crept to the front. He could see shapes of bushes… was that someone moving? He was glad he could hear Randy and Amy giggling from inside the house— at least they hadn't missed him and come looking for him.

Jay looked again at the bushes near the front of the house. Was that someone crouched down? Jay held his breath and made no sound. And no sound came from behind the bush. He waited some more, breathing as slowly and as quietly as possible.

Jay was determined to make his way to the bush and see for himself if she was there.

Cindy desperately wanted to peek outside and see what was happening. Had Jay found Claudia? Was he in trouble? She started marching toward the windows,

hoping to catch a glimpse of something, anything.
"March, march, march!" she said as she clapped in
time. Randy and Amy and Dexter were right behind
her. Dexter knew what Cindy was trying to do. He
wanted to look out the windows too without alerting
the children to any danger.

The New Rule

It seemed to be taking so long, Cindy thought. She worried about Jay. What if he'd cornered Claudia? What would she do? Cindy finally caught a glimpse of him crouching near a bush. He was alone. Or was Claudia hiding behind the bush?

CHAPTER 8

Noises in the Night

WHAT TIMING. JAY couldn't believe that he had to sneeze. He pressed the ridge under his nose the way Cindy had told him to if he didn't want to sneeze, but he still felt it tingling. He pressed harder. The sneeze went away. Jay smiled smugly in the dark. Heart pounding, he made a sudden decision to leap behind the bush and confront Claudia.

Cindy and Dexter, still marching in place with the children, watched Jay outside the window. They watched him leap behind the bush, yelling "Gotcha!"

But Jay came up empty. There was no one there. He'd been so sure. Then where was she? He ran to the bush on the other side of the sidewalk. No one. He looked around the yard, near the porch. No other places to hide here, just trees lining the street. Could they have been mistaken? As if to ask Cindy and Dexter, he looked in the window. He saw them both shrug questioningly.

After Jay had checked the entire yard and found that no one was hiding anywhere, he came back inside.

"Thought I had her," Jay said, shaking his head.

"We sure thought she was out there," Dexter said.

"Who? Who? Who?" asked Randy, still marching in place.

"You're an owl, Randy," Amy said happily. "I know about owls. They hoot."

Cindy was glad for the distraction and knew she would have to talk to Jay later. There was so much to talk about! If only the Spotlighters could check on the cemetery right now. She wondered if Claudia had heard anything and where she was. Well, they'd just have to be patient. They would have to wait until Mr. Maxwell got home in an hour.

The wait seemed endless. The Spotlighters did their best to entertain Amy and Randy, but their hearts weren't really in it.

At last, they heard the familiar tap on the horn from Mr. Maxwell's car as he drove it into the garage. In a moment he joined them in the living room, carrying a newspaper. "Didn't see this before," he said. "Must have delivered it late."

"Hi, Dad," Randy chirped. "What happened with the ducks?"

Mr. Maxwell chuckled. "All lined up, Randy."

"Did they quack?" asked Amy.

"Sure did," he said with a smile. Then he turned to the Spotlighters. "Thanks so much for watching the kids for me,"

"Our pleasure," Cindy said. She could barely stand in one spot she was so eager to leave.

"And thanks for getting them into their pajamas."

"Sure," she said. She was surely going to jump out of her skin.

Mr. Maxwell reached into his pants pocket and came up with a few bills. "Here you go, kids. I really appreciate it." Jay pocketed the money and would split it up later.

By the time they left the Maxwell house, it was past dusk, and the shadows on the street weaved in and out of the lampposts. The Spotlighters were beside themselves with excitement...and the need to talk.

"So Claudia wasn't in the yard," Jay said.

"What was that thump?" asked Dexter.

Jay shook his head. "I didn't see anything unusual," he said. "I just don't know."

"Maybe we'll never know," Cindy said.

"*I* can't believe how lucky we are that we had to babysit Amy and Randy tonight," Jay said, hopping on his bike.

"I'll say," Dexter added. "We'd still be clueless." He waited on his bike for Cindy to get on hers.

"Let's just hope it's where the kids said it is," Cindy said. She was about to get on her bike when she stopped suddenly. "Shhh!" she whispered to the boys. "There's something out there!"

Jay and Dexter froze where they were. Cindy's hand was raised as if to ward off something heading her way.

"I still think Claudia is trying to follow us," she said.

There was a soft rustling somewhere behind the Spotlighters. They waited in silence. The rustling continued.

"I heard something," Cindy whispered. "I'm sure of it."

"What did it sound like?" Jay whispered back.

"Like sneaking," Cindy answered.

"Sneaking?" Dexter repeated.

"Like someone—Claudia—was trying to sneak up on us," Cindy affirmed. She put her finger to her lips and waited. There was no more rustling. Just a soft breeze floating through the trees.

"I don't think she's there," Jay said, his voice normal. "Just like in the yard at the Maxwells'."

"I just had a feeling..." Cindy trailed off. She still didn't get on her bike.

"There's just something..." her voice was small. The boys respected her concern and waited.

After a few minutes, Cindy shook her head. "Must have been an old raccoon or something," she said half-heartedly.

Noises in the Night

"Yeah," Dexter agreed.

"But...but ...is anyone besides me worried about Claudia and what she might do?" she asked. "I mean, maybe she did follow us to the Maxwells'...and waited. She could be out there somewhere right now, watching us from behind a tree or something."

"She's nowhere near us," Dexter assured her. "I have a special kind of radar for things like that."

"Well, I sure hope you're right," Cindy said.

"Of course," Dexter said. "Remember the time we were working on the newspaper mystery and you and Jay were absolutely positive no one was around? And I wasn't so sure... I felt someone nearby. And sure enough, someone was hiding under the desk the whole time. And I'm pretty sure it works the other way too. I don't feel that anyone's sneaking up on us."

"Okay," Cindy said uncertainly. "If you're sure."

Dexter shook his head. "It's just a feeling," he said. "Like the way you feel something in your bones. I guess we have to trust our instincts."

"That's what I thought I was doing," Cindy protested. "In fact, I still feel uneasy. But I'm going to forget about it so we can get to the cemetery and find the locket."

"Now you're talking," Jay said. "Let's go."

"Should we split up?" Cindy asked.

"Nah" Jay said. "This is too important. "The three of us should be together."

"Right," Dexter and Cindy said together. On their bikes, the Spotlighters rode quickly to the cemetery. The night was dark and moonless. Clouds blocked out the stars, and it was cool again. Shadows played among the trees, making the cemetery seem alive. They parked their bikes near the front gate and walked in. A lone owl hooted in the distance.

The Spotlighters looked at each other, each of them remembering the night they'd heard the whispered voice pierce the darkness. Tonight was like that night—still, cool, dark.

Cindy tried to shake off the feeling that clung to her still—that Claudia after all might be following them. She tried her best to focus on the important thing— the locket. And they were so close to finding it!

"How many hitching posts are there?" Jay asked.

Noises in the Night

"Twelve," Dexter reminded him.

"Let's go," Cindy said.

It wasn't long before they reached one of the hitching posts. The air was still, and there was a chill that seemed to wrap itself around the Spotlighters.

"I can't believe how real the horse's head looks," Cindy said. "It almost looks like his ears twitched."

"You're giving me the willies," Jay said. "It's enough having Chuck believe in ghosts."

"I'm just teasing, silly," Cindy said. "But it does look real."

"What is real is that the vase isn't here," Dexter said. "Let's find the next hitching post."

They continued on, the night settling more deeply around them. They suddenly heard a strange noise behind them and stopped. Holding their breath, the Spotlighters stood stock-still. They heard it again. Jay shone his flashlight on the ground and gasped when an opossum scuttled by, trying to avoid the light.

"It's just an animal," Jay said reassuringly. "Just an old opossum." But Cindy could tell by his voice that he'd been scared for a minute. Well, so had she.

By the time they reached the eighth post, they were feeling discouraged.

"Maybe somebody came by and took it," Dexter worried.

"Claudia," Cindy suggested. "She probably was hiding outside the Maxwells' when we were there with Amy and Randy—she probably heard everything. And sneaked up here before we had a chance."

"I don't think so," Jay said. "Look over there." He

Noises in the Night

was pointing to a hitching post—and something glinted near the ground.

Cindy sucked in her breath. "I hope you're right, Jay!"

The Spotlighters crowded near the hitching post. And indeed, there was the vase, filled with flowers. Just as Amy and Randy had described.

"I can't believe it," Cindy breathed. "The vase. We actually found it!"

"You do the honors," Dexter insisted. "You're the one who found the mystery in the first place."

Heart pounding, Cindy reached down to lift the vase. It was heavier than she expected. She gently removed the flowers and turned to the boys. "Here goes," she said, tipping the vase upside down.

The locket fell to the grass without a sound. "We've got it!" Dexter nearly shouted. The Spotlighters gazed at the locket for a long moment. Jay broke the silence with a whoop as Cindy picked up the locket and clutched it in her hand. The Spotlighters instinctively hugged each other, clapping each other on the back. "Wait," Cindy said. "I have to open it. Serafina wrote that her father was handsome. I want to see that for myself." It took a little time but Cindy was able to use her fingernails to open the locket. "Look, here he is—Will Winslow! And he was quite good-looking."

"And that mustache is pretty amazing too!" chuckled Dex.

"We've got to get back and call Carmen," Cindy said breathlessly. She quickly put the flowers back in the vase and set it back down where it had been.

Noises in the Night

For safekeeping, Cindy gently put the locket around her neck. She felt special wearing Serfina's necklace... and even more special thinking of Will Winslow's making it so long ago.

The Spotlighters ran back to their bikes and sped home in the dark. Cindy didn't once think of Claudia. The night was beautiful and friendly and wonderful, Cindy thought.

The first thing she did when she got home was to get Carmen's number. She dialed.

"Two rings...three rings...four rings," she said, looking at the boys. She waited another minute and then slowly hung up the phone. "She's not there," she said.

"We'll keep trying," Jay assured her.

"In the meantime, I'm getting my notebook," Cindy said with determination. "And Serafina's journal."

Just then Mrs. Temple came in from the living room with a big bowl of popcorn. "Oh good, you're home. Save me from eating all this popcorn—I can't eat another bite."

"Fine with me," Dexter said. "I'll help."

"How were Amy and Randy?" asked Mrs. Temple.

"Very helpful," Jay said cryptically.

"Oh?"

"Oh, Mom, we found Carmen's locket!" Cindy said happily. "Thanks to the kids."

"How wonderful!" Mrs. Temple said with a smile.

"We're just about to write everything down in my notebook," Cindy said.

"While we eat popcorn," Dexter added.

"There's lemonade in the fridge," Mrs. Temple said. "I'll leave you to your mystery while I finish my book."

CHAPTER 9

The Black Horses

CINDY TOOK THE locket off from around her neck and studied it. It was even more beautiful than she'd remembered it. She passed it to Jay.

"There's not a mark on it," he marveled. He passed it to Dexter, who first wiped his glasses on his shirt. "I wonder how Will Winslow managed to make this inscription so unusual—it really looks like it's lighted from behind or something."

"I noticed the same thing," Cindy said. "It must be a trick of the light."

"However he did it," Dexter mused, "I've never seen anything like it before."

"Here's the drawing Serafina drew of it," Cindy said, turning the journal around so it faced the boys.

They whistled in unison. "It looks so real," Jay said.

"Like a photograph," Dexter agreed. "She sure was a good drawer."

"An artist, just like her father," Cindy said with admiration. She opened her notebook.

"This locket," she said. "What is it about it that is so unusual? We know it's important, of course. It's made by Will Winslow and therefore probably worth quite a bit of money. But beyond that . . ." She cleared her throat. "Query: What is special about this locket? Answer: It holds a secret. Serafina didn't know what it was."

"Maybe Claudia does," Dexter said slowly. "What if she knew we had it?"

A sudden dark cloud filled Cindy. She remembered the terrible, sudden anger that had come over Claudia during the yard sale. Would Claudia do something to the person who had the locket? It was the same unease she had felt at the Maxwells' and when she and Jay and Dexter had left them, thinking that maybe Claudia was hiding nearby.

She thought of Carmen. "Maybe we should keep

this quiet," she thought aloud. "Not let anyone know yet that we have the locket." She looked at the boys, waiting for their opinions.

"I think you're right, Cindy," Jay said after a moment. "We don't know what Claudia is capable of. And until we know more, we should definitely keep this information to ourselves."

Dexter nodded solemnly.

Cindy breathed a sigh of relief. She glanced down at Serafina's journal, turning it to face her again. She munched a handful of popcorn. In a moment she turned to the boys.

"There's something in this journal leading us to an answer," she said.

"But what kind of answer?" Jay asked. "I don't have a clue what we're looking for. At least when we didn't have the locket, I knew what we were looking for."

"Okay," Cindy said. "What have we got? I'd better write it down." She started to make a list. "What are all the things we've run into with this mystery? Let's try to think of everything."

"Well, ghosts," said Dexter.

"We didn't actually run into any," Cindy said.

"But it's part of the mystery," Dexter insisted. "And Chuck believes in them. He's part of it. He's the one who told us all about Will Winslow."

"Okay, okay, you're right," Cindy relented. "I'm writing ghosts down. What else?"

"The locket," Jay said. "Claudia, Carmen."

"Right," Cindy said, neatly writing her list.

"Serafina's journal," Dexter said.

"The bench in the cemetery," Jay added.

Cindy wrote busily and then sat back to see what she had written. "There's plenty here, especially considering the journal and what is in there that we haven't really seen." She tapped her pen on her notebook. "We know the locket has a secret. That's something."

"Then we should read the whole thing," Dexter said.

"Or maybe we should concentrate on today," Cindy wondered. "What is it about the locket today that's so important? Or is it important at all except for the fact that Claudia wants it?"

"Well, since Will Winslow made it, it's very valuable," Jay said. "That makes it important."

The Black Horses

"Everything he made is valuable and important," Dexter added.

"True," Cindy said. "But is that why Claudia wants the locket? Or is it for another reason? And if so, what?"

She stared at Serafina's journal and finally picked it up. "It's in here," she said. "Somehow, our answer is in here."

That night while Cindy slept, her dreams were filled with black horses. She dreamed that she had her own stallion, a sleek and muscular steed that seemed to understand her every thought. They rode together through fields and forests, exploring everything. In her dream, they stopped at a bench, and Cindy hopped off, admiring its handsome work. Her horse nuzzled her and then nuzzled the bench. The horse seemed to be trying to tell her something.

And then Cindy woke up. No, no, she didn't want to wake up from such a dream…she tried to fall back asleep but it was too late. She was truly awake. It was a funny feeling, wanting to be asleep in her dream more than she wanted to be awake. Like most dreams, this one seemed to fade from the edges of her mind as soon as she climbed out of bed and moved around. What was that part about the bench? Cindy shook her head. It was just a dim sliver of memory.

Over breakfast, she and Jay and Dexter talked about Carmen. Cindy worried that the locket should be returned to her as soon as possible but also worried about what Claudia might do if she knew.

"I'm with keeping our mouths shut," Dexter said. "It's safer that way."

"I'm with Dex," Jay said. "The same as last night."

Cindy shook her head. "I feel funny," she admitted. She touched the locket around her neck. "Almost as if I've stolen it or something."

"That's ridiculous!" Jay sputtered. "You've found a valuable locket that you're safekeeping! You're doing the right thing!"

Cindy looked at Jay. "In my head, I know you're right," she said. "It's my heart that messes things up."

Dexter shook his head. "Let's go back to where we were—trying to figure out what is so important about the locket."

"Okay," Cindy said, rubbing her temples as if to

clear her head. "Maybe if we read some more of Serafina's writings, something will click."

She once again pulled Serafina's journal in front of her and picked a passage to read aloud. "Midnight... oh, Midnight. Such a fine specimen of a horse. And he is all mine. Papa made a trade with a local farmer, and I am to take care of him. I shall feed him and brush him and ride him. I shall ride him everywhere."

Cindy put the journal down. "This is really weird," she said, feeling a strange sensation of déjà vu. "I had this dream last night...I had my own black stallion, and I was riding and riding. And there was something else." She shook her head. "It seemed important in my dream," she said.

"Dreams," Jay said. "I don't get them. Some seem like a regular day, going to school or cutting grass or walking on the sidewalk, and then there's the one where you find yourself on a boat in some wild river and you're sure you're gonna tip over and drown."

"I could spend days just dreaming," Dexter said. "I like strange ones where you suddenly fall into the sky and can't get down...zooming farther and farther away..."

Cindy laughed. "I wouldn't trade dreams with you for anything," she said. "But I know what you mean. Strange and mysterious things go on in dreams. Maybe when I grow up I'll write a book about them."

"If anyone writes about them, it'll be you," Mrs. Temple said as she entered the kitchen. "Morning, kids! I once dreamed that I found a kitten. The very next day when I opened the porch door, there was a kitten, mewing and mewing. It was almost like a premonition."

"What's a premonition?" asked Jay.

"It's when you think of something before it happens," Mrs. Temple said.

"Like a prediction?" asked Dexter.

"Sort of," smiled Mrs. Temple.

"I dreamed something last night that I wish I could remember," Cindy said. "I do remember riding a beautiful horse...but there was something else."

"Maybe some pancakes would help," offered Mrs. Temple. "With butter and syrup—and a little bacon on the side."

"I can't possibly say no," Dexter said, "even though we already had cereal."

The Black Horses

"Sounds too good to pass up," said Jay.

"I thought I was full," Cindy said. "But the mere mention of butter and syrup on pancakes...I could drool."

As Mrs. Temple fixed the pancakes and bacon, Uncle Dan came in the kitchen. "Something smells awfully good in here. Yum." He poured himself a cup of coffee and sat down at the table with the Spotlighters.

"There's a pretty interesting article in this morning's paper," he said, spreading it out in front of him. "Thought you three would be particularly interested, since you've done so much to help the museum."

The Spotlighters looked at Uncle Dan and waited.

"'Random Street Fund-Raiser Not Enough,' is the headline," Uncle Dan read. He looked at Jay, Cindy, and Dexter. "Want to hear more? It's not encouraging."

"Yes!" Cindy insisted.

"Okay," Uncle Dan said. "Here goes: 'In spite of the good intentions of local citizens, the effort to raise funds to save the museum from closing failed, forcing the board to hold an emergency meeting to discuss the details of the closing.'"

"Wow," breathed Jay. "That's terrible. I can't believe it."

"Me either," said Cindy. A sinking feeling flooded her whole being. "Now what?" she asked.

Uncle Dan shook his head. "I'm afraid there's nothing to be done, to tell the truth." He rested his elbows on the table. "You know, that great old museum has been around since way before I was a kid," he said. "It's sad."

"Why, it's just terrible," said Mrs. Temple, bringing the platter of pancakes and bacon to the table. "I remember having my tenth birthday party there. There was a new exhibit of wolves and coyotes and foxes, and we were just thrilled." She smiled, remembering. "They were all stuffed, of course, but looked so real… we were quite enchanted." Then she frowned. "And to think that now kids won't have that opportunity. It's just awful."

Except for the occasional clattering and scraping of forks on plates, the kitchen was silent.

"Well, this won't do," said Uncle Dan, interrupting the Spotlighters' gloomy silence. "Let's have a rousing game of Scrabble after breakfast." Neither Jay, Cindy, nor Dexter volunteered.

"Okay," said Uncle Dan. "How about a rousing bike ride? Anywhere you want to go."

"I'm sorry, Uncle Dan," Cindy finally volunteered. "I really don't feel like either. I just want to figure out about the locket."

"Me too," said Jay and Dexter together.

"I know when I'm not wanted," Uncle Dan chuckled, picking up his plate from the table. "I'll clean up in here while you detectives get to work."

Mrs. Temple smiled and joined him at the sink.

In minutes, the Spotlighters had forgotten that Uncle Dan and Mrs. Temple were still in the kitchen.

"Let's look at Serafina's drawings," Dexter suggested. "That should get our minds off the museum."

CHAPTER 10
The Key to the Mystery

"HERE'S THE LOCKET," she said. "All views. Sideways, frontways, backward…and the words, of course, *Love is the Key*."

The Spotlighters stared at the drawings, intent on seeing something they hadn't seen before. What, though? Cindy flipped through more pages, passing drawings of the lampposts, headstones, squirrels…and the drawings of the bench. The intertwining leaves… the intertwining hearts on the side of the bench, where Cindy had run her fingers over a hundred times.

"Where's the locket?" Jay suddenly asked. "I'd like to look at it again." Cindy carefully removed it from

The Key to the Mystery

her neck and handed it to Jay. "I should really put it in a safe place," she said. "But I feel so special wearing it."

Jay turned it over in his hands, looking at it from every angle. "Love is the Key," he said.

"Keys open things," Dexter said.

Cindy suddenly drew in her breath. "Wait a second. Oh my gosh, wait a second." She reached for the journal and looked at the drawings of the bench. She hurried to another page where Serafina had written, "When I figure out the secret, Papa says that things will have come full circle. I do not know what that means."

"What are you thinking?" Jay asked, holding the locket in midair.

"The locket," Cindy said breathlessly. "The locket is a key itself. And it opens something…something that Serafina has drawn, something we know." She stared at the boys.

"The bench," she whispered.

"What?" Jay said. "What are you saying?"

"Yeah, what are you saying?" Dexter said, pushing his glasses up.

"The locket is a key itself," Cindy said excitedly. "That's the secret. And it unlocks something in the bench."

"The bench?" asked Jay. "How could it do that?"

"I don't know," Cindy said. "But I know it does. Look here." She pointed to a passage in Serafina's journal. "Papa told me that it is a very special piece, even more special than just for sitting on. He loves to pose riddles." And then there was the long arrow that pointed to the two intertwined hearts.

"I don't get it," admitted Dexter.

"The lock is the key that unlocks something in the intertwined hearts of the bench," Cindy said. "This is the answer to the puzzle!"

Jay and Dexter stared at each other and then back at Cindy. "What are we waiting for?" exclaimed Jay.

"Let's go!" Dexter said.

"Bye, Mom! Bye, Uncle Dan!" said Cindy. "We'll be back later!"

Mrs. Temple and Uncle Dan could only stare after the Spotlighters, who were already leaping on their bikes outside.

The Key to the Mystery

Their hearts were pounding by the time they reached the cemetery. "Wait till we tell Carmen," Cindy said, out of breath.

They sped to the bench, their hearts in their throats. The sun was shining and the trees still had glistening dew on them. It was a beautiful morning. The Spotlighters carefully set their bikes down and gathered together, not paying attention to their surroundings.

"Have you got the locket?" Jay asked Cindy.

"Of course," Cindy replied excitedly. She gently unclasped it from around her neck and looked at it in the sunlight. Not just a locket. A key.

"I'll take that!" shrilled a sharp voice suddenly behind them. Claudia, appearing without warning at their sides, reached for the locket. "I knew you had it, I just knew it!" she shrieked at Cindy. "This locket is mine! I shall own everything it stands for! You will not! Give it to me and stand out of my way! You're nothing but a conniving, snively thief!"

Cindy gasped in astonishment and disbelief. Her forebodings had been right after all. Claudia had been on her trail. She looked miserably from the locket in her hand to Claudia's pinched face and her reaching hand.

"Not so fast," came a familiar voice. It was Chuck, hedge trimmers in hand, arriving at that moment. "These are my friends," he said in his clipped voice. "You don't look like one." He reached Cindy and Jay and Dexter and stood between them and Claudia, his feet planted firmly on the grass. The locket was still in Cindy's hand, twinkling in the sun.

"This—this is an outrage!" screamed Claudia, still trying to reach the locket, Chuck in her way. Her pointed fingers clutched at the air. She tried batting Chuck out of the way and grabbing the locket, but she was getting nowhere. Spittle formed at the edges of her mouth as she tried to shift her body one way and then another. And then, with a final, wretched howl of anger, she spun away and fled.

The Spotlighters watched her retreat and then looked gratefully at Chuck. "How did you just happen to be here when—?" Jay started to say.

"Luck," Chuck said. "This is where I head early in the morning, one of my favorite spots." He paused.

The Key to the Mystery

"Like you, Cindy. What's going on? Who was that miserable woman?"

Cindy explained as best she could about Claudia and the locket. And why all the Spotlighters were here at the bench. "It's all part of our mystery. Remember when I said we were detectives?"

Chuck nodded.

"Well, we're solving a mystery right now." She pointed to the locket. "And this has been a big part of it." Chuck watched in fascination as Cindy bent toward the bench with the locket.

She looked for and found the intertwined hearts on the side. "It's right here," she said. "This is where the locket goes." She took the slim locket and brought it near to the hearts. Where to insert it? And then she saw a nearly invisible line between the hearts...this must be where.

The boys crowded close to her as she pushed the locket into the slim recess...and pushed it a little bit more. And suddenly there was a heavy thunk as a small iron drawer eased itself out of the side of the bench.

The Spotlighters stared. Chuck gasped. The little

drawer was about the size of a deck of cards. And inside this drawer was a piece of paper…and something wrapped in a little bit of cloth.

When Cindy didn't make a move to do anything, Jay nudged her with his elbow. "Let's see what's in here," he whispered. It was broad daylight, and no one was around, but it seemed the right thing to do, whisper.

"Okay," Cindy said. "First let's see what's in the cloth." She slowly and carefully reached in the box and picked up the cloth-wrapped object. The cloth fell away to reveal a delicate and beautiful silver ring. Faintly, the initials *WW* were inscribed on the edge. And inside the ring itself were the words *Love Lasts*.

Jay, Cindy, and Dexter looked at each other.

"Holy cow, Chuck, this is the ring you were talking about!" Dexter exclaimed. "Old Will really did make it after all."

Chuck was obviously overcome with emotion and was speechless.

Cindy hardly knew what to think. She looked at the piece of paper still in the box and drew it out. It

was surprisingly sturdy, considering how old it must have been. She opened it. In a sprawling penmanship, she read, "I, Will Winslow, being of sound mind, declare that all my earthly possessions shall belong to Kenoska..." There were more words, but Cindy stopped.

"Serafina never knew...never opened this secret box, never got her ring. So when Will Winslow said that things have come full circle, back to the very beginning, he meant the ring. He made it when he was very young, knowing that he would love someone in the future, someone he would want to have the ring. And that person, in the end, turned out to be Serafina. And the words *Love Lasts* are the words he meant for Serafina all those years ago." Cindy blinked.

The boys were quiet for a moment. Chuck hadn't spoken at all. Now he did. "You three have accomplished a miracle," he said. "This is the best Will Winslow news I've ever heard." He shook his head. "I can't even think straight I'm so flabbergasted." He looked again wistfully at the ring, shaking his head. "After all my time cleaning up the bench, admiring

The Key to the Mystery

Will Winslow's work, being a part of all of it, I never in a million years would have guessed what you three figured out. Never."

"Well," Cindy said. "We may not have gotten this far if you hadn't intervened when Claudia was here, trying to get the locket away from us."

"I think we need to tell Carmen about everything first," Jay said. "It's her locket, after all, and she's the one who—"

As if by magic, Carmen suddenly appeared. Her eyes were red, as if she'd been crying. "I can't believe you're all here," she said, a little out of breath. "I just wanted to come by and think things through—I'm still so upset about all of the family things...Claudia, the locket..." She hesitated and then went on. "And the oddest thing! I just saw Claudia. She was in a wild state, muttering and swearing, pulling at her hair. I thought she was going to attack me or something, she looked so angry, but I guess she just didn't see me."

"She was here," Jay said. "She wanted to take the locket from us."

"But Chuck saved the day," Cindy interrupted.

"And we found what the locket opens," Dexter said.

Carmen stared at the Spotlighters. "You can't mean that you actually found the locket!" she squealed. "And what do you mean, 'what the locket opens'? And who's Chuck?"

"You're looking at a trio of the cleverest kids in Kenoska," Chuck said proudly. "I'm Chuck." He held out his hand and shook Carmen's.

"He wouldn't let Claudia take the necklace from us," Jay said again. "So Cindy was able to use the locket to open a secret compartment that Will Winslow had made many many years ago for Serafina."

"The locket is a key?" Carmen asked, dumbfounded.

The Spotlighters nodded. "And that's all thanks to Serafina's journal and her drawings, really," said Cindy. "They helped us figure everything out. She was quite a talented artist."

"So the locket is a key," Carmen said, shaking her head. "And you discovered not only that but that it

The Key to the Mystery

opened a special compartment. And you found out where the compartment was! I'm just mind-boggled."

"Me too, ma'am," Chuck admitted.

"I wonder if Claudia knew about the locket's being a key," mused Jay. "She sure was eager to have it. After all, she'd been wearing it even before you came back to town."

"How could she possibly have known?" Carmen asked. "It's obvious that she had no use for the old box of things from the attic. She never read Serafina's journal."

"Or did she?" asked Cindy. "Maybe she just pretended not to be interested in any of it when in fact she knew all about it."

"But if she knew anything, why wouldn't she have found what you did?" wondered Carmen. There was a heartbeat of silence, and then Carmen asked, "What did you find?"

The Spotlighters sat on the bench with the little compartment and showed Carmen the ring from inside. Gently, tenderly, Carmen lifted the ring out and studied it. Chuck leaned over her shoulder to look at it again as well. "This is beautiful," she said. "Just beautiful." She turned the ring over in her hands and read, *Love Lasts*. "This ring says it all. About the whole Winslow family."

"Except for Claudia," Jay said. "I think she wanted the locket out of spite."

"Spite," nodded Cindy. "How unlike the ring in the secret box."

"And it isn't all that was in the box," Dexter offered.

Carmen looked curiously at the Spotlighters and at Chuck. "Another surprise?" she asked. "I've never known so many twists and turns!"

"This final twist is the best of all," declared Cindy. "Your ancestor left all of his belongings to Kenoska."

There was another silence, and it was louder than any silence Cindy had ever heard. She looked at Carmen.

"All of Will Winslow's works?" Carmen whispered. Her gaze drifted over the Spotlighters to the sleek hitching posts and back to the bench. "There's so much everywhere!"

"More than anybody in Kenoska knows," Chuck said proudly. "Now we'll really be on the map. For all time!"

114

The Key to the Mystery

"And here," said Cindy. "This is yours—finally in your hands." And she handed the locket to Carmen, who took it and held it to her cheek for a moment before thanking the Spotlighters for everything. "Honestly, I never thought I'd see it again," she said. "And here it is, more beautiful than ever."

Later, after all the explaining and describing and remembering, the Spotlighters felt like celebrities. They certainly were treated like ones. The headline in the following day's newspaper read, "Local Trio of Kids Saves Museum!" And there followed a story about how the single ring they'd found in the secret compartment was worth enough money to not only save the museum but rebuild major portions of it as well. And the will of Will Winslow, declaring all his work donated to Kenoska, made Kenoska a very wealthy town indeed.

"I wonder what's going to happen to Claudia," Jay mused, after all the excitement had died down for a while and he and Cindy and Dexter were saying good-bye to Carmen, who was leaving town.

"I guess no one's seen hide nor hair of her since

she left the cemetery in such a state," Carmen said. "I think she's gone for good."

Cindy smiled at Carmen. "Well, she left that old house with everything in it...maybe you should consider moving in."

"I might just do that," Carmen said with a twinkle in her eye. "I might just do that."

**Check Out More Exciting Mysteries
from Albert Whitman & Company!**

Discover more
Spotlight Club Mysteries!

Why would anyone break into a bookmobile—but take nothing? Someone is looking for a secret among the stacks and it's up to the Spotlight Club to figure out the truth…

Albert Whitman & Company
albertwhitman.com

One warm night four children stood in front of a bakery. No one knew them. No one knew where they had come from.

Edgar® Award-winning Series!

The Buddy Files

He's a dog. He's also a detective!

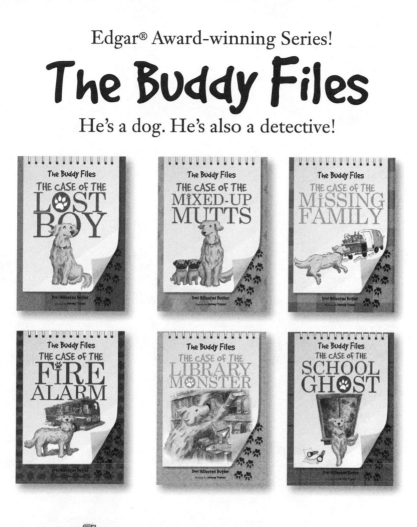